GHOULIA

GHOULIA

AND THE GHOST WITH NO NAME

Book 3

Text and illustrations by Barbara Cantini
Translated from the Italian by Anna Golding

Amulet Books
New York

Cataloging-in-Publication Data has been applied for and may be obtained from the Library of Congress.

ISBN 978-1-4197-4688-8

Text and illustrations by Barbara Cantini
Original Italian title: *Mortina e l'amico fantasma*
© 2018 Mondadori Libri S.p.A.
Translation by Anna Golding
Art Director for original Ghoulia series: Fernando Ambrosi
Graphic Designers for original Ghoulia series: Marina Bassi and Stefano Moro

Book design by Max Temescu and Jade Rector

Printed and bound in China
10 9 8 7 6 5 4 3 2 1

ABRAMS The Art of Books
195 Broadway, New York, NY 10007
abramsbooks.com

To those who are no longer here but remain with me forever

I would like to thank my editor, Sara Di Rosa, for her dedication and hard work as well as everyone else who worked on the Ghoulia series, especially Stefano Moro, Marta Mazza, and Manuela Piemonte. I also want to thank professor Cristina Giorgetti for teaching me so much about costume design and fashion. Finally, thank you to my family, who walk by my side with happiness, patience, and support.

—B. C.

The Residents of

GHOULIA

AUNTIE DEPARTED

TRAGEDY

SHADOW

Crumbling Manor

GRANDAD COFFIN

PET WORM

ROTTEN

UNCLE MISFORTUNE

New Year's Eve

THE GHOST

MICHAEL

BRUNO

Party Guests

SARAH

JOHNNY

THERESA

At the end of December, Crumbling Manor was covered in a layer of snow. All was calm and peaceful as the residents of the manor anticipated the annual "Dead But Not Departed" New Year's Eve Party.

Ghoulia played vampires with Tragedy

and had snowball fights with her friends from the village.

One night, she heard noises on the roof. Just a split-second before he vanished, Ghoulia spotted a boy sitting on a fresh patch of snow. He was glowing, too!

Is Placid sleeping or frozen?

My mother
as a child

Granny
Coffin

The next morning, Uncle Misfortune
was furious because something—or perhaps
someone?—had disturbed the ash in his
fireplace, covering the room in dark black soot.

It's 6 o'clock

Comedy, Tragedy's father

Later that evening, Ghoulia was reading *The Ghost of Cantinville* to Tragedy when a tap at the living room window made her jump.

They curiously peered out the window and discovered a shining ghost boy waiting outside! He was a little faded and frowning slightly.

"Let me in!" he commanded, panicked.

"What's wrong?" Ghoulia asked, waving him
in out of the cold.

"I don't have anywhere else to go. I refuse to
go back into the black hole!" he replied.

Rotten
investigates

"What's your name?" asked Ghoulia.
"I don't know. I can't remember."
"You've lost your memory!" Ghoulia cried.
The boy explained that he could only remember
that he had lived in the village and he was eight
years old when he died. He told them he had
been trying to enter Crumbling Manor for days.

"*You're* the glowing light! And I'll bet you covered Uncle Misfortune's room with soot, trying to sneak in through the chimney," said Ghoulia, putting all the pieces together. "But our house is protected by a magic spell, so no one can enter unless we invite them inside. Not even ghosts. Where did you come from?"

The ghost told his story. He had been trapped in a hole in a tree in the garden. Once inside, he started to disappear completely! But he had narrowly escaped.

"I'm not sure how I found my way to the tree,
but I'm never going back! It's dark, and it smells
like rotten eggs!"

Ghoulia wanted to help this nice ghost boy.
She decided to ask for advice from the ghost she
knew best: Grandad Coffin!

"Who's there? Does anyone want to play a rousing
game of chess?" yawned Grandad Coffin,
who had clearly been napping.

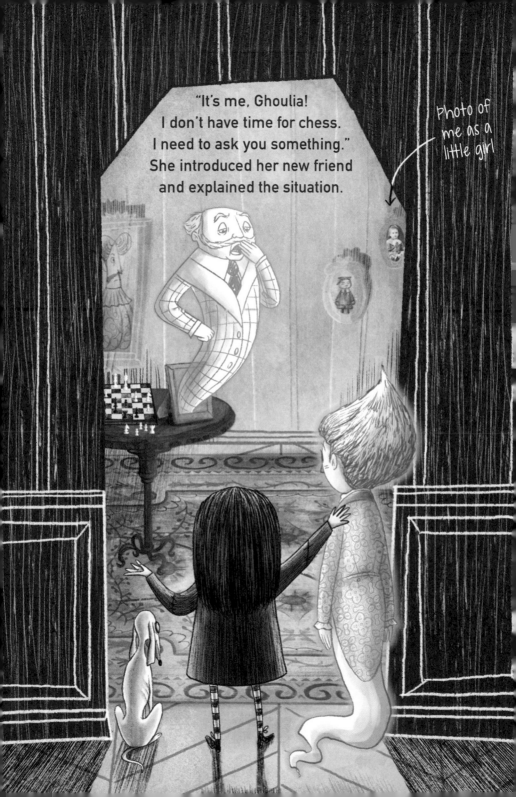

Crow →

Grandad Coffin told them about Oblivion,
a place for ghosts who have lost their memories.
Creatures who have been completely forgotten
go to Oblivion to disappear.

"But I had no idea we had a portal to Oblivion
in our own garden," said Grandad Coffin.

"I think the only way to stop your friend from disappearing is to discover his lost name, and then to never forget it. I am safe from Oblivion because you and Auntie Departed remember me. So you can remember your friend, too!" concluded Grandad Coffin.

Who are you?

Grandad Coffin

Ghoulia

ny Coffin

Me as a three-year-old

Uncle Misfortune as a boy

?

Auntie Departed

Auntie Ann

Misfortune

Tragedy is a very accomplished photographer!

It was time to get to work.
"Let's go to the library!"
Ghoulia exclaimed.

"We already know *where* you're from. So now
we'll need to figure out *when* you're from," said Ghoulia.
She consulted a book called
Fashion Design Through the Centuries.

Little helper

Ghoulia carefully studied the boy's outfit from head to
toe. She and Tragedy figured out what material was
used for the jacket, the trousers, and the waistcoat.

After an hour of research, they deduced that the ghost boy was born sometime around 1810.

Portrait of his Lordship (always sad)

One of my drawings

But how would they find his name?

Auntie's ancient pot

Uncle Misfortune's favorite drink

RAT

VERMI SECCHi

Rotten Lettuce Pie

100 PARTY IDEAS

Guest list

Ghoulia set off to find Auntie Departed to see if she had any ideas about how to solve the mystery. She knew Auntie would be in the kitchen, preparing the menu for the "Dead But Not Departed" New Year's Eve Party planned for that weekend.

Fig mustard from 1902

Auntie Departed was in the kitchen, but she had been distracted by one of Uncle Misfortune's pet worms, who had escaped from Misfortune's hat. (There was always something unexpected going on in Crumbling Manor!)

FLOUR

Auntie Departed and her sour lemon face!

(A sour lemon)

After Ghoulia filled her in on the mission to find the ghost's lost name, Auntie Departed told her all about the church register. Anyone looking for details about someone from the past could check there to find records of births, weddings, and funerals.

But Auntie Departed told Ghoulia that she must not enter the village church because she might be spotted. "It's absolutely out of the question!" she cried, with a sour face.

Ghoulia promised Auntie Departed she would not go to the church under any circumstances! At the same time, she crossed her fingers and hatched a plan. She would leave the ghost with Tragedy and sneak out through her bedroom window later that night.

Ghoulia grabbed a dark hooded cape so that she could stay hidden. She decided to drop down slowly so that she wouldn't make much noise.

First, she let down one foot . . . then the other . . . next her legs . . . and her torso . . .

Travel sewing kit

. . . and finally, hugging her head in her arms, she spun to the ground, landing in the soft snow.

After stitching herself back
together, Ghoulia sped off
toward the church!

A full moon lit up the churchyard, bathing it in a blue
light and casting dark shadows on the snowy ground.
A light shone from the caretaker's window, but outside
there was total silence.

Ghoulia pushed the gate open, and it creaked loudly—
too loudly! The caretaker poked his head out of the
window and called, "Is anyone there?"

Meeeoooooow!!!

Ghoulia pretended to be a cat,
and the caretaker closed his window.

Ghoulia carefully entered the candlelit church. She walked down the aisle and headed straight for the office where the records were kept. She scanned the names of everyone born between 1805 and 1820.

Fortunately, the village was very small, and Ghoulia was very determined. Unfortunately, Ghoulia heard a door creak open before she found her friend's name . . . Anthony, Anna, Alice, Maria, Rebecca, Ricky . . .

She grabbed the register and slipped out of the office. She was hoping to dash up the aisle and out the front doors, but the caretaker was approaching too quickly. She needed to hide *now*! Ghoulia jumped into an empty coffin waiting for its "guest."

The caretaker entered the room, humming and muttering to himself. "Oh no! I thought this coffin was empty. Why is it the wrong size? And it's such a shame they've made such a mess of the makeup. She's all purple . . ." Ghoulia just couldn't help herself.

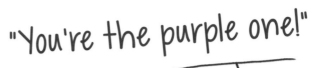

"You're the purple one!"

she shouted,
sitting upright in the coffin.

Aaaaaah!!!

The caretaker cried out, then fainted, his face as white as a ghost.

Escape!

Ghoulia leaped from
the coffin and dashed
back to Crumbling Manor
with the register tucked
under her arm.

When she was back inside Crumbling Manor,
Ghoulia searched through the records with the ghost
boy until they finally discovered his name: Nicholas.

Nicholas

Dragon

rotten

Idea for
a dress

Amelia Departed

rotten's
home

Once he rediscovered his name,
Nicholas's memories came flooding back.
He shined brightly once again, and Ghoulia
found him frightfully cute!

"We must find a way to make sure
you never forget your name again!"
said Ghoulia.

She sifted through Uncle Misfortune's
treasures to find two lockets.

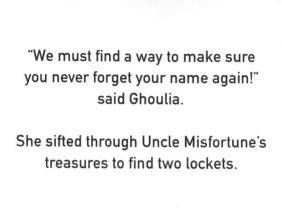

On two pieces of paper, she wrote
"Nicholas." She put one in each locket.
She hung one around her neck and said,
"I will remember you forever."

She gave the other locket to Nicholas and said, "Now you will always remember your name . . . and you will always remember me. I've included my photo as well . . ."

"Thank you, Ghoulia!" Nicholas beamed.

Auntie's false teeth

Auntie has very big feet →

Moldy mints

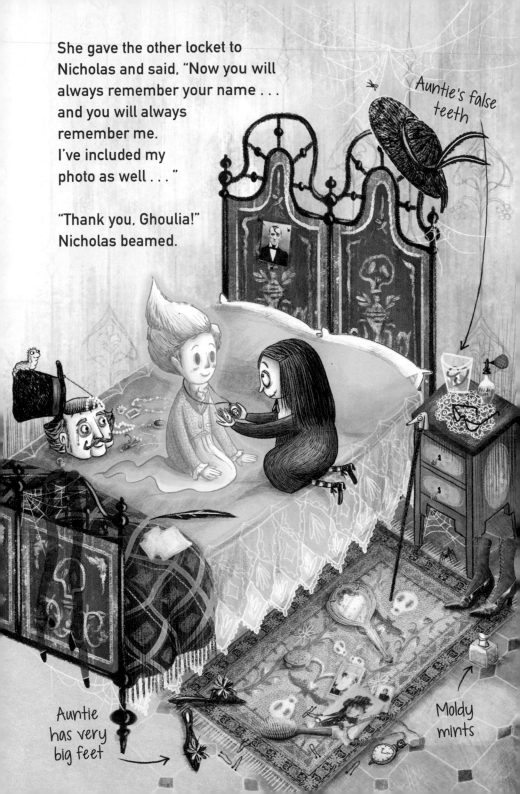

"Since you don't have anywhere to be . . . why don't you stay here with us? The day after tomorrow we are hosting our annual "Dead But Not Departed" New Year's Eve Party. All of my friends from the village will be here. There will be dancing and lots of food!" Ghoulia really didn't want Nicholas to leave.

Nicholas happily accepted the invitation.
He felt very at home at Crumbling Manor, and
Ghoulia got a shining escort for the party.

The party quickly kicked up into full swing!
Uncle Misfortune sang loudly with a musical quartet.
They were his bandmates from the old days.
(The very, very old days!)

Uncle Misfortune sang so loudly, in fact,
that his pet worm ran away for good.

Everyone was dressed up in their finest clothes. Auntie Departed wore an old hat topped with a birdcage, complete with a real singing blackbird!

Annoyed worm

Ghoulia wore an old dress in her signature color (purple!) that had belonged to her Granny Coffin. It really brought out the circles under her eyes.

Original dress from 1863

. . . a few tears and moth holes

All her friends from the village had worn their best clothes, too. When they saw the food prepared by Auntie Departed, they decided it was better to spend their time dancing.

The best dressed of all was Tragedy, in a suit and top hat. He danced the night away with Theresa.

"I think this year will be the best yet!" Ghoulia
said, spinning around the dance floor with
her new friend Nicholas.

Turn the page for some
extra-special fun!

Nicholas's
Memory Game

Look at this photo long and hard and
commit as much as you can to memory.
On the next page, you'll need to
answer questions about it.

How much do you remember?

1. Who is sitting on the bed?

2. What color is Ghoulia's blanket?

3. What side of the room is Rotten's mousehole on?

4. Is Nicholas in the image?

Design a special party outfit!

Ghoulia and Auntie Departed throw their "Dead But Not Departed" New Year's Eve Party every single year. And this year, you're invited! What will you wear?

On the next page, Ghoulia has gathered all of the best party clothes from around Crumbling Manor.

Using a piece of tracing paper, build your outfit piece by piece. You might choose to pair the dress with the top hat or the waistcoat with the boots. Don't be afraid to mix it up!

HAVE NO FEAR!

Ghoulia will soon return
for another adventure.

GHOULIA

AND THE DOOMED MANOR

Barbara Cantini